HORRID HENRY
Tricks the Tooth Fairy

HORRID HENRY
Tricks the Tooth Fairy

Francesca Simon
Illustrated by Tony Ross

Orion
Children's Books

ORION CHILDREN'S BOOKS

Horrid Henry Tricks the Tooth Fairy originally appeared in the
black and white storybook of the same title
first published in 1997 by Orion Children's Books
This edition first published in Great Britain in 2013
by Orion Children's Books
This edition published in 2016 by Hodder and Stoughton

10

A CIP catalogue record for this book is available from the British Library.

ISBN 978 1 4440 0115 0

Printed and bound in China

The paper and board used in this book are from well-managed forests and other responsible sources.

Orion Children's Books
An imprint of Hachette Children's Group
Part of Hodder and Stoughton
Carmelite House
50 Victoria Embankment
London EC4Y 0DZ

An Hachette UK Company
www.hachette.co.uk
www.hachettechildrens.co.uk

www.horridhenry.co.uk

For Josh,
who inspired this story

There are many more **Horrid Henry** books available.

For a complete list visit

www.horridhenry.co.uk

or

www.orionbooks.co.uk

Contents

Chapter 1

"It's not fair!" shrieked Horrid Henry. He trampled on Dad's new flower-bed, squashing the pansies. "It's just not fair!"

Moody Margaret
had lost two
teeth.

Sour Susan
had lost three.

Clever Clare lost
two in one day.

Rude Ralph had lost four, two top
and two bottom, and could spit to
the blackboard from his desk.

Greedy Graham's teeth were
pouring out.
Even Weepy William had lost one –
and that was ages ago.

Every day someone swaggered
into school showing off a big black
toothy gap and waving fifty pence
or even a pound that the
Tooth Fairy had brought.

Everyone, that is, but Henry.

"It's not fair!" shouted Henry again.
He yanked on his teeth.
He pulled, he pushed, he tweaked,
and he tugged.
They would not budge.
His teeth were superglued
to his gums.

"Why me?" moaned Henry,
stomping on the petunias.
"Why am I the only one who hasn't
lost a tooth?"

Horrid Henry sat in his fort
and scowled.

He was sick and tired of other kids
flaunting their ugly wobbly teeth
and disgusting holes in their gums.

The next person who so much as mentioned the word 'tooth' had better watch out.

Chapter 2

"HENRY!"
shouted a squeaky little voice.
"Where are you?"

Horrid Henry hid behind
the branches.
"I know you're in the fort, Henry,"
said Perfect Peter.
"Go away!" said Henry.

"Look, Henry," said Peter. "I've got something wonderful to show you."
Henry scowled. "What?"
"You have to see it," said Peter.

Peter never had anything good
to show.

His idea of
something
wonderful was
a new stamp,

or a book
about plants,

or a gold star
from his teacher
saying how
perfect he'd been.

Still…
Henry crawled out.
"This had better be good," he said.
"Or you're in big trouble."

Peter held out his fist and opened it.
There was something small and white
in Peter's hand. It looked like …
no, it couldn't be.

Henry stared at Peter.
Peter smiled as wide as he could.
Henry's jaw dropped.
This was impossible. His eyes must be playing tricks on him.
Henry blinked.
Then he blinked again.

His eyes were not playing tricks. Perfect Peter, his *younger* brother, had a black gap at the bottom of his mouth where a tooth had been.

Henry grabbed Peter.
"You've coloured in your tooth with black crayon, you faker."

"Have not!" shrieked Peter.
"It fell out. See."
Peter proudly poked his finger
through the hole in his mouth.
It was true. Perfect Peter had lost
a tooth. Henry felt as if a fist had
slammed into his stomach.

"Told you," said Peter.
He smiled again at Henry.

Henry could not bear to look at Peter's gappy teeth a second longer. This was the worst thing that had ever happened to him.

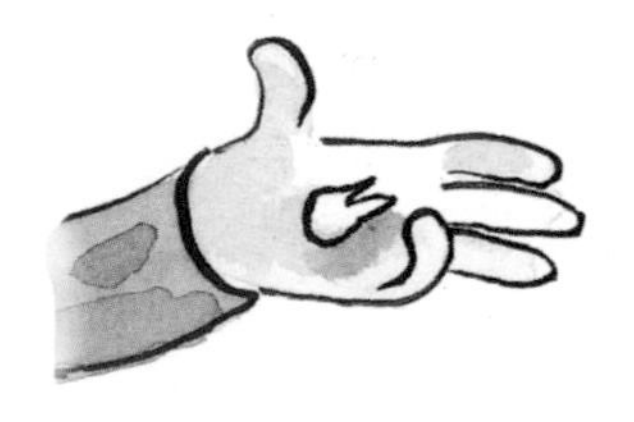

Chapter 3

"I hate you!" shrieked Henry. He was a volcano pouring molten lava on to the puny human foolish enough to get in his way.

"AAAAGGGGHHHH!" screeched
Peter, dropping the tooth.

Henry grabbed it.

"OWWWW!" yelped Peter.
"Give me back my tooth!"

"Stop being horrid, Henry!"
shouted Mum.

Henry dangled the tooth
in front of Peter.
"Nah nah ne nah nah," jeered Henry.

Peter burst into tears.
"Give me back my tooth!"
screamed Peter.

Mum ran into the garden.
"Give Peter back his tooth this minute," said Mum.

"No," said Henry.

Mum looked fierce.
She put out her hand.
"Give it to me right now."

Henry dropped the tooth
on the ground.
"There," said Horrid Henry.

"That's it, Henry," said Mum.
"No pudding tonight."
Henry was too miserable to care.

Peter scooped up his tooth.
"Look, Mum," said Peter.

"My big boy!"
said Mum, giving him a hug.
"How wonderful."

"I'm going to use my money from the Tooth Fairy to buy some stamps for my collection," said Peter.

"What a good idea," said Mum.
Henry stuck out his tongue.

"Henry's sticking out his tongue
at me," said Peter.

"Stop it, Henry," said Mum.
"Peter, keep that tooth safe for the
Tooth Fairy."

"I will," said Peter.
He closed his fist tightly
round the tooth.

Chapter 4

Henry sat in his fort.

If a tooth wouldn't fall out,
he would have to help it.
But what to do? He could take
a hammer and smash one out.

Or he could tie string round a tooth, tie the string round a door handle and slam the door.

Eek!

Henry grabbed his jaw.

On second thoughts, perhaps not.
Maybe there was a less painful way
of losing a tooth.
What was it the dentist always said?
Eat too many sweets and your teeth
will fall out?

Henry sneaked into the kitchen.
He looked to the right.
He looked to the left.

No one was there. From the sitting room came the screechy scratchy sound of Peter practising his cello.

Henry dashed to the cupboard where Mum kept the sweet jar.

Sweet day was Saturday, and today was Thursday. Two whole days before he got into trouble.

Henry stuffed as many sticky sweets into his mouth as fast as he could.

Chomp

Chomp

Chomp

Chomp.

Chomp

Chew

Chomp

Chew.

Chompa Chew
Chompa Chew.

Chompa...
Chompa...

Chompa...
Chompa...

Chew.

Henry's jaw started to slow down.
He put the last sticky toffee in
his mouth and forced his teeth
to move up and down.

Henry started to feel sick.
His teeth felt even sicker.
He wiggled them hopefully.

After all that sugar one was sure to fall out. He could see all the comics he would buy with his pound already.

Henry wiggled his teeth again.
And again.
Nothing moved.

Rats, thought Henry.
His mouth hurt.
His gums hurt.
His tummy hurt.
What did a boy have to do
to get a tooth?

Chapter 5

Then Henry had a wonderful, spectacular idea. It was so wonderful that he hugged himself.

Why should Peter get a pound from the Tooth Fairy? Henry would get that pound, not him.

And how?
Simple.
He would trick the Tooth Fairy.

The house was quiet.
Henry tip-toed into Peter's room.

There was Peter, sound asleep,
a big smile on his face.
Henry sneaked his hand under
Peter's pillow and stole the tooth.

Tee hee, thought Henry.

He tiptoed out of Peter's room
and bumped into Mum.

"AAAAGGGHH!" shrieked Henry.
"AAAAGGGHH!" shrieked Mum.

"You scared me," said Henry.

"What are you doing?" said Mum.

"Nothing," said Henry.
"I thought I heard a noise in Peter's
room and went to check."

Mum looked at Henry.
Henry tried to look sweet.

"Go back to bed, Henry," said Mum.

Henry scampered to his room and put the tooth under his pillow. Phew. That was a close call. Henry smiled. Wouldn't that cry-baby Peter be furious the next morning when he found no tooth and no money?

Henry woke up and felt under his pillow. The tooth was gone. Hurray, thought Henry.

Now for the money.

Henry searched under the pillow.
Henry searched on top of the pillow.

He searched under the covers, under
Teddy, under the bed, everywhere.
There was no money.

Henry heard Peter's footsteps
pounding down the hall.
"Mum, Dad, look," said Peter.
"A whole pound from the
Tooth Fairy!"

"Great!" said Mum.

"Wonderful!" said Dad.

What?! thought Henry.

"Shall I share it with you, Mum?" said Peter.

"Thank you, darling Peter, but no thanks," said Mum. "It's for you."

"I'll have it," said Henry. "There are loads of comics I want to buy. And some—"

"No," said Peter. "It's mine. Get your own tooth."

Henry stared at his brother. Peter would never have dared to speak to him like that before.

Horrid Henry pretended he was a pirate captain pushing a prisoner off the plank.

"OWWW!" shrieked Peter.

"Don't be horrid, Henry," said Dad.

Henry decided to change
the subject fast.

"Mum," said Henry.
"How does the Tooth Fairy *know*
who's lost a tooth?"

"She looks under the pillow,"
said Mum.

"But how does she know whose
pillow to look under?"

"She just does," said Mum.
"By magic."

"But how?" said Henry.

"She sees the gap between your teeth," said Mum.

Aha, thought Henry.
That's where he'd gone wrong.

That night Henry cut out a small piece of black paper, wet it, and covered over his two bottom teeth. He smiled at himself in the mirror. Perfect, thought Henry.

He smiled again.

Then Henry stuck a pair of Dracula teeth under his pillow. He tied a string round the biggest tooth, and tied the string to his finger.

When the Tooth Fairy came, the string would pull on his finger and wake him up.

All right, Tooth Fairy, thought Henry.
You think you're so smart.
Find your way out of this one.

Chapter 6

The next morning was Saturday. Henry woke up and felt under his pillow. The string was still attached to his finger, but the Dracula teeth were gone. In their place was something small and round...

"My pound coin!" crowed Henry.

He grabbed it.
The pound coin was plastic.

There must be some mistake, thought Henry. He checked under the pillow again. But all he found was a folded piece of bright blue paper, covered in stars.

Henry opened it.
There, in tiny gold letters, he read:

"Rats," said Henry.

From downstairs came the sound
of Mum shouting.
"Henry! Get down here this minute!"

"What now?" muttered Henry,
heaving his heavy bones out of bed.

"Yeah?" said Henry.

Mum held up an empty jar.
"Well?" said Mum.

Henry had forgotten all about
the sweets.
"It wasn't me," said Henry
automatically. "We must have mice."

"No sweets for a month," said Mum.
"You'll eat apples instead.
You can start right now."

Ugh.

Apples.
Henry hated all fruits and vegetables,
but apples were the worst.

"Oh no," said Henry.

"Oh yes," said Mum. "Right now."

Henry took the apple and bit off the teeniest, tiniest piece he could.

CRUNCH.
CRACK.

Henry choked. Then he swallowed, gasping and spluttering. His mouth felt funny.

Henry poked around with his tongue
and felt a space.
He shoved his fingers in his mouth,
then ran to the mirror.

His tooth was gone.
He'd swallowed it.

“It’s not fair!”
shrieked Horrid Henry.

What are you going to read next?

More adventures with

Horrid Henry,

or go to sea with

Poppy the Pirate Dog,

or into space with

Cudweed.

You could have fun on

A Rainbow Shopping Day,

or explore

Down in the Jungle,

but watch out for
A Creepy Crawly Story!
Make magic with
The Three Little Witches,
and have a ball with
Princesses.
Or follow the star in
The First Christmas.
Enjoy all the Early Readers.